This fun-a-rooney
Annual 2004
belongs to

....

Lost Toys

Izzles has hidden something belonging to each of the
Tweenies and to Doodles on some pages in this annual.
Look for the toys as you read. The answers are on page 61.

Milo's
car

Fizz's
balloon

Bella's
xylophone

Doodles'
ball

Jake's
wheelbarrow

First published in 2003 by BBC Worldwide Limited
Woodlands, 80 Wood Lane, London W12 0TT
2 4 6 8 10 9 7 5 3 1
Text by Sally Foord-Kelcey
'Makes' devised by Natalie Abadzis
Illustrations by Alan Craddock, Stephanie Longfoot, Magic Island,
Maggie Sayer and Bill Titcombe
Photography on pages 16-17, 30-31, 42-43 and 54-55 by Christopher Baines
With thanks to Jade, Xavier, Harriet and Saoirse
Design by Smiljka Surla
Text, design and illustrations © 2003 BBC Worldwide Limited
Tweenies © 1998 BBC
Tweenies © 1999 BBC Worldwide Limited
Tweenies is produced by Tell-Tale Productions for the BBC
CBeebies & logo ™ BBC. © BBC 2002
Printed and bound in Singapore
ISBN 0 563 49106 X

Tweenie clock – where will it stop?

Come on everybody! Let's sing
Five Little Men in a Flying Saucer

Five little men in a flying saucer
flew round the world one day.
They looked left and right,
but they didn't like the sight.
So one man flew away.

Four little men in a flying saucer
flew round the world one day.
They looked left and right,
but they didn't like the sight.
So one man flew away.

Three little men in a flying saucer
flew round the world one day.
They looked left and right,
but they didn't like the sight.
So one man flew away.

Two little men in a flying saucer
flew round the world one day.
They looked left and right,
but they didn't like the sight.
So one man flew away.

One little man in a flying saucer
flew round the world one day.
He looked left and right,
and he did like the sight.
So this man came to stay.

7

All Aboard the Tweenies' Starship

"Telly time," shouted Milo. Judy was showing the Tweenies a video about stars and planets.

"Where are the aliens, Judy?" asked Milo.

"If you watch very carefully you might see an alien or two," said Judy, with a twinkle in her eye.

She pointed out some planets in the sky. There was a red planet called Mars, an enormous planet with stripes and a spot called Jupiter and one with rings around it called Saturn.

"Can't see any aliens, though," giggled Milo.

"Oh, look! There's a rocket. And some people are getting into it," said Jake.

"They're called astronauts," Bella told him.

"What's that big blue and green ball, Judy?" asked Fizz.

"It's planet Earth, where we live," Judy replied. "That's what it would look like if you were high up in the sky."

Then Judy had an idea. "Why don't we make our own planets?" she suggested. "We could make a rocket, too," said Jake, "and go on a journey into space." So Milo, Bella and Fizz made planets at the messy table...

...while Judy and Jake made a rocket out of a big box.

When they had finished, Judy hung the planets from the ceiling, and Jake climbed into his rocket.

"All aboard the Tweenies' starship," Captain Jake called, and together the Tweenies zoomed up, up, up into the sky.

"Keep a look out for aliens, everyone," called Milo.

They saw some strange planets on their journey. One was stripy, one was spotty and one was speckled. Another had flowers all over it. There was even a checked planet.

9

The Tweenies pretended they were inside a spaceship. Suddenly they heard a strange noise.

"What's that?" said Fizz, feeling a bit scared.

"Captain Jake, there's something on the screen," said Bella.

"Wow, aliens!" cried Milo. "Fab-a-rooney!"

The aliens were jumping up and down, squeaking and squawking and babbling.

"I think they need our help," said Bella.

"You'd better whoosh them on board," commanded Captain Jake.

So Bella pushed the whoosh pad.

WHOOOSH!

Five aliens appeared inside the spaceship – a speckled one, a checked one, a stripy one, a flowery one and a spotty one.

The flowery alien explained, "Our rocket is broken and we can't get home to our planets."

"Is there anything you can do?" asked the spotty alien.

"Please? Pleeease?" pleaded the stripy one, the checked one and the speckled one.

"Don't worry. The Tweenies' starship to the rescue!" cried Jake. "We'll soon get you home."

"Prepare the whoosh pad," said Milo.

"Three, two, one, GO!" shouted Fizz.

Bella pushed the whoosh pad.

WHOOOSH!

One by one, the aliens got whooshed back to their matching home planets – a stripy planet, a checked one, a flowery one, a spotty one and a speckled one. And everyone was very happy.

"Mission complete," said Captain Jake.
"Time to go home," said Bella. "Ready?"
Then she pushed the whoosh pad one more time.

WHOOOSH!

The Tweenies' starship sped back to planet Earth.

"That was fun," laughed Fizz. "But it's good to
be home."

THE END

Bella's Fun Page
Hi! I'm Bella.

Join the dots to write my name.

I like dressing up, so today I'm pretending to be an astronaut.

I like making things, too. We made six planets when we played spaceships. Spot the matching pair.

1

2

3

5

4

6

I've drawn a rocket. Colour it in for me. My favourite colour is red.

Answer: 1 and 4.

13

Flying Machines

The Tweenies have been talking about *machines that fly*.
Judy is going to show them a video about an air show that she
and Jake visited. Can you find Judy and Jake in the air show picture?

Match the little
pictures to the
big picture.

biplane
This plane has two
sets of wings and a
propeller engine.

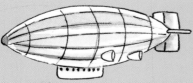

airship
This has a balloon filled
with special gas to help
it float.

helicopter
This can fly straight
up, down, forwards,
backwards or sideways.

hot air balloon
This has a basket
for passengers.

aeroplane
This passenger plane
has two jet engines.

parachute
With one of these,
people can jump safely
from planes.

Space Station Boomerang

Throw this space station boomerang like a frisbee, and it will skim gently through the air and fly back to you. Ask a grown-up to help.

You will need:
Tracing paper
Pencil
Coloured card
Round-ended scissors
Black pen
Small, round, coloured stickers

1 Place the tracing paper over the template and copy the lines in pencil. Turn over the tracing paper and scribble over the lines on the back. Then place the tracing paper the right way up on a piece of card. Pressing hard on the pencil, draw over the lines.

2 Cut out the boomerang and the hole in the centre.

3 Use the black pen to draw space
station windows around the hole
on the central part of the boomerang.

4 Put two rows of small,
round, coloured stickers
along each arm of the boomerang.

5 Now throw the boomerang like
a frisbee and watch it come back
to you.

Template

We Love Animals

The Tweenies love animals. They like animal books and toys, making and drawing animals, even pretending to be animals!

Look at the picture carefully and answer the questions.

Who can climb trees?

Who has eight arms?

Who has a trunk?

Who hisses?

Count how many of these animals are in the picture.

butterflies

chicks

seahorses

lions

parrots

Answers: The octopus has eight arms. The monkey can climb trees. The elephant has a trunk. The snake hisses. 4 butterflies, 3 chicks, 3 seahorses, 1 lion, 2 parrots.

Where's My Mummy?

Can you help the babies find their mummies?
Draw lines between them.

lion

chick

puppy

duck

duckling

dog

cub

bird

Mix-and-Match Animals

You've never seen animals like some of these!

Ask a grown-up to help you cut along the two dotted lines on this page and on page 23. Then flip the different sections of the pages.

p
e
n
k
e
y

You're driving me bananas!

21

Bathtime!

l i p h a n t

Elephantastic!

22

Have another!

m o n g u i n

Fish is my favourite dish!

23

I'm not scared!

That's what they all say.

24

Rainforest Search

Look very carefully at these two rainforest scenes.
Can you spot five differences between them?

Answers: In the second picture there is another toucan, another parrot, another butterfly, another flowering branch and another toadstool.

:

ignore

x
story time

Wings

One day, Fizz put on her butterfly outfit because she felt like looking pretty.

Bella wanted to look pretty, too, so she looked in the dressing-up box.

"Just you watch, mate," Milo said to Jake. "Any moment now Bella will come out wearing a tutu with a tiara on her head. She'll say..."

"...Da da! I'm a beautiful princess," Jake continued.

"Da da! I'm a beautiful princess," cried Bella, as she stepped through the curtains.

Jake and Milo thought they would dress up. Fizz the Butterfly was in the garden when Milo the Eagle and Jake the Pirate appeared.

"What shall we play?" asked Jake.

"Well," said Fizz. "I'm a butterfly with big coloured wings. And Milo's a bird with big feathery wings..."

"And I'm a pirate," said Jake.

"So you're the odd one out," Milo told him. "We have wings so we can play flying. Go find some wings."

Jake looked in the dressing box, but he couldn't see any wings, so he wandered off to find Doodles.

Meanwhile, Bella was reading a book about a mouse, and decided to dress up as a pretty little mouse.

"Ooooh, you look so sweet," cried Fizz, as Bella the Mouse stepped into the garden.

"Mice haven't got wings, so you can't play flying with us – unless you turn into a bat," Milo giggled.

Bella wanted to play flying, so she found a piece of velvet for bat wings.

But where was Jake?

"I suppose he could join us later," said Fizz.

Bella, Milo and Fizz flapped their wings as they ran round and round the garden. They sang a song:

"Wings, wings are wonderful things,
They let you fly so high.
Gently flap them up and down.
Soon you're swooping over the town,
Up into the clear blue sky."

They had got to the top of the climbing frame.

"It's really windy up here," said Bella. "I can't fly properly anymore."

"We've flown too high," said Fizz. "We're stuck here until someone rescues us."

Indoors, Jake was telling Doodles how he wished he could play flying with the others but he couldn't because he had no wings.

"Be Dotman," said Doodles.

"Of course," cried Jake. "Silly me! Dotman's a superhero. He hasn't got wings but he can fly!"

Jake put on his Dotman cape and raced outside.

"Help!" he heard Milo calling.

"We're stuck on top of the mountain. It's too windy to fly down."

"Do not fear, Dotman's here. I'll fly you all to safety," yelled Dotman.

Then, one by one, he led the Tweenies safely down the slide.

"Thank you, Dotman," said Bella. "You're a hero."

"A superhero," said Dotman.

THE END

27

Colouring In

Colour in this picture of the Tweenies
wearing their flying costumes.

Lion-in-a-Cheese-Box Card

Surprise your friends when you give them this card!

Ask a grown-up to help.

You will need:
Round, flat cheese box with a lid
Yellow and brown card
Pencil
Black pen
Round-ended scissors
Paintbrush
Yellow paint
Safe glue
Ruler

1 Place the lid on the yellow card and draw a circle around it. Do this again to make another circle. Draw two ears, four legs and a tail on the yellow card, using the photographs of the finished card as a guide. Cut out all the pieces.

2 To make the lion's mane, place the lid on the brown card and draw a circle around it. Draw a wavy line around the outside of the circle. Cut out the mane along the wavy line. Snip along the wavy line with scissors to make a fringe. Draw a smaller circle 1cm inside the first circle, and cut out the smaller circle to make a hole.

3 Use the paintbrush and yellow paint to paint around the side of the base and the side of the lid. Glue two legs onto the lid of the box and the other two onto the base. Then glue one yellow card circle onto the top of the lid and the other one onto the bottom of the base.

4 Glue the mane onto the yellow circle on the lid. Glue on the two ears. Use the black pen to draw on a lion's face. Glue the tail onto the middle of the base.

5 To make the stretchy lion's body, cut out two strips of yellow card each 7cm x 84cm. Glue them together to make an L shape.

6 Fold one yellow strip over the other. Keep going until you reach the ends of both strips and have made a concertina.

7 Glue one end of the concertina inside the lid and the other end inside the base. Close the cheese box, write a message beside the lion's tail and give it to a friend!

messy time

Milo's Fun Page
Hi! I'm Milo.

Join the dots to write my name.

I like animals. Here I am with two of my favourites.

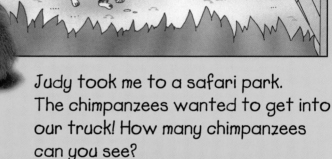

Judy took me to a safari park. The chimpanzees wanted to get into our truck! How many chimpanzees can you see?

This is a picture of the animal I'd most like to meet. A scary-a-rooney stegosaurus! Colour it in for me.

32

Answer: There are six chimpanzees.

Up-and-Down Puzzle Page

1 What's going up in this picture? Who's going down?

2 All these things can go up in the sky, except one. Spot the odd one out.

bat

ostrich

butterfly

aeroplane

3 This grows up and down. Colour in the shapes with a dot to find out what it is.

Answers: Puzzle 1: The ball, skipping rope and kite are going up. Jake is going down.
Puzzle 2: The odd one out is the ostrich, which is a bird that can't fly.
Puzzle 3: A tree. The roots grow down, while the trunk and branches grow up.

33

Come on everybody! Let's sing
I Wish I Could Bounce
on a Pogo Stick

I wish I could bounce on a pogo stick,
boinging up and down!
Bounce like me on my pogo stick,
boinging up and down.

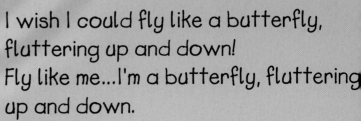

I wish I could fly like a butterfly,
fluttering up and down!
Fly like me...I'm a butterfly, fluttering
up and down.

34

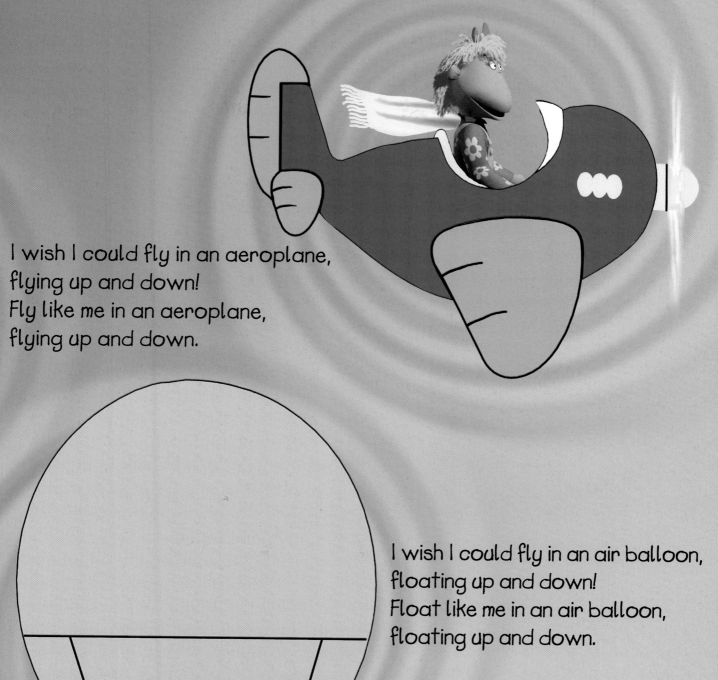

I wish I could fly in an aeroplane,
flying up and down!
Fly like me in an aeroplane,
flying up and down.

I wish I could fly in an air balloon,
floating up and down!
Float like me in an air balloon,
floating up and down.

I'm Stuck!

The Tweenies were playing an up-and-down game in the garden.

"Look at me," yelled Milo. "I'm really high up."

"Weeeeee! I'm sliding down," cried Jake.

"Woof! Woof!" barked Doodles. "I want to go up the climbing frame and down the slide."

But every time Doodles tried, somebody stopped him.

"You can't go up the steps," said Fizz.

"It's my turn next," said Bella.

"I'll never get a turn," Doodles grumbled, and walked off.

The Tweenies liked their up-and-down game.
But they stopped when they heard Doodles barking.
The Tweenies looked all over the garden.
   "Doodles, Doodles, Doodles," they called.
   Then Fizz spotted him.

   Doodles was up in a tree!
   "Come down," called Milo.
   "I'M STUCK!" howled Doodles.
   "We've all got to think of ways to get Doodles down," said Bella.
   "Maybe he should flap his ears and fly," Jake said.
   Milo wished he had his pogo stick so he could bounce up to Doodles and bring him down.
   "We could chop down the tree!" said Fizz.
   She went to fetch Max.
   Doodles lifted his ears and began to whine.

Max thought axes were dangerous and, anyway, why did Fizz want to chop down the tree?

"Because Doodles is stuck in it!" Fizz replied. "Look!"

"Oh dear," said Max. "Cats usually get stuck in trees."

"GET ME DOWN!" howled Doodles.

"Wait a minute," said Max, and he went back indoors.

"I expect he's gone to get an aeroplane," Bella said.

Max returned with a long ladder. He set it against the tree and climbed up, up, up...

"Come on, boy," he said when he reached the top.

Then he scooped Doodles under his arm and together they climbed down, down, down the ladder to the ground. Doodles shook himself with relief.

"Thank you, Max," he said.

But later on, when the Tweenies were indoors telling
Max all about their up-and-down day, they heard
Doodles barking again.

"I'm stuck!" he howled.

Everyone rushed into the garden, just in time to see
Doodles whizzing down the slide.

"Only kidding!" he laughed.

THE END

Colouring In and Dot-to-Dot

Jake and Bella are playing another
up-and-down game.

Jack and Jill
went up the hill
to fetch a pail of water.
Jack fell down,
all the way down,
and Jill came tumbling after.

Join the dots to find the pail of water. Draw the water spilling out of it
and colour in the picture.

41

Up-and-Down Doodles Puppet

Make Doodles' ears move
up and down.
Ask a grown-up to help.

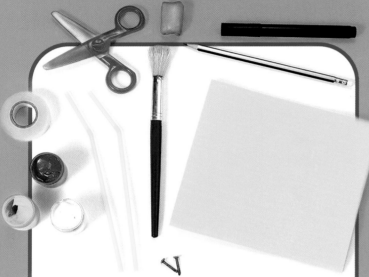

You will need:
Flat kitchen sponge
Black pen
Round-ended scissors
Red, yellow and white paint
Paintbrush
Pencil
Two paper fasteners
Two bendy drinking straws
Sticky tape
Re-usable adhesive

1 Using the photograph of the finished puppet as a guide, draw a Doodles head and body shape, and two ears, onto the sponge.

2 Draw Doodles' face on his head, and paint him on both sides.

42

3 Make holes for the paper fasteners. First, make holes through the wide ends of the ears with the tip of the pencil. Then place the ears either side of the head. Push the pencil through the holes in the ears, and keep pushing so that you make holes in the head, too. Use re-usable adhesive to keep the ears and the head steady while you make the holes.

5 Cut about 2.5cm off the drinking ends of the straws. Bend over the drinking ends and tape them to the back of the puppet's ears.

6 Take a straw in each hand and move them up and down. Doodles' ears will go up and down, too!

4 Push one paper fastener through each ear and the head. Turn the puppet over and bend the paper fasteners' legs to secure the ears in place.

43

Fizz's Fun Page
Hi! I'm Fizz.

Join the dots to write *my* name.

I like playing up-and-down games, and I like drawing. Do you like *my* picture of a kite going up and down?

Help the goats find the way up and down this *mountain*.

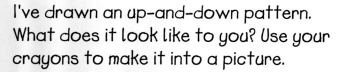

I've drawn an up-and-down pattern. What does it look like to you? Use your crayons to make it into a picture.

44

Who Am I?

The Tweenies, Doodles and Izzles like trying out different costumes.
Match the pictures of them to the silhouettes.

Answer: 1 = d, 2 = f, 3 = b, 4 = a, 5 = c and 6 = e.

The Magic Lamp

story time

One day, Judy came in with a box holding some coloured beads, a sparkly ring, a golden crown, a long black cloak and a silver teapot.

Bella had an idea. "Do you remember that pantomime we saw about Aladdin and the magic lamp?" she asked. "Let's act out the story! Aladdin's in it, and his mum, his wicked Uncle Abanazar, a wicked servant, a beautiful princess and two genies."

"Can I be Uncle Abanazar?" asked Jake. "I'm feeling wicked today."

So Jake was Uncle Abanazar, Doodles was his wicked servant, Bella was both genies, Milo was Aladdin and Fizz was the princess

and Aladdin's mum. The silver teapot was the magic lamp. Max and Izzles watched the play, while Judy told the story.

Once upon a time there was a boy called Aladdin who lived with his mum. She wished they were rich so she didn't have to work so hard. One day, Aladdin's wicked Uncle Abanazar came to visit.

46

Uncle Abanazar took Aladdin for a walk to a deep, dark cave. Now, Abanazar wouldn't go inside the cave because it had magic powers and could destroy wicked people. But inside the cave was something that could make him rich and powerful.

"Listen, Aladdin," he said. "I want you to bring me the old lamp from inside this cave."

He threw Aladdin a sparkly ring and pushed him into the cave.

Aladdin could hardly believe his eyes. The cave glittered with gold and jewels.

"Wow! Glitter-ooney!" said Aladdin. Then, "Found the lamp!" he called.

Abanazar wanted Aladdin to give him the lamp before he left the cave, but Aladdin wouldn't. Abanazar tried to climb into the cave to grab the lamp, but a huge stone rolled in front of the entrance and, with a puff of smoke, he disappeared. Poor Aladdin was trapped inside the cave! His fingers rubbed against the sparkly ring and suddenly there was a terrific WHOOSH!

"I am the Genie of the Ring," said Bella. "What is your wish, oh master? But make it quick. It's cold in this cave."

"OK," said Aladdin. "I wish I was back home."

The Genie clapped her hands and in a flash, Aladdin was at home with his mum. He told her what had happened.

"I don't know why Abanazar wanted this old lamp," said Aladdin, rubbing it with his sleeve. Then there was another terrific WHOOSH!

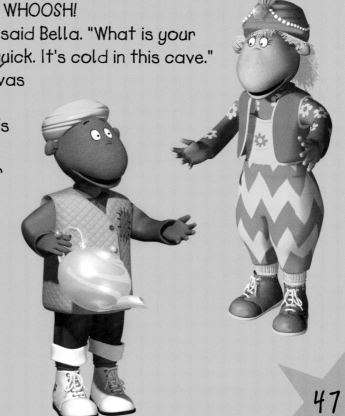

"Now I'm the Genie of the Lamp," said Bella. "What is your wish, oh master?"

Aladdin wished to become a rich man so his mum didn't have to work so hard. He wished to marry a beautiful princess and live in a palace. Presto! The Genie granted all his wishes.

"Oh, Aladdin!" said the princess. "Aren't you going to kiss your bride?"

"No way!" said Aladdin. "That's not in my story!"

One day, the princess heard someone shouting outside the palace gates, "New lamps for old!"

She decided to swap Aladdin's old lamp for a nice new one. Little did she know that the lampseller was really Uncle Abanazar.

As soon as he had the lamp in his hands Abanazar laughed loudly.

"You silly princess. Now I have you in my power!" he said.

He rubbed the lamp and the Genie appeared.

"I am the Genie of the Lamp," said Bella. "What is your wish, oh master?"

"Take the princess to my house. That'll show Aladdin who's boss," ordered Abanazar.

The Genie clapped her hands.

When Aladdin found out that his wife and the lamp had disappeared, he guessed it was the work of Abanazar. So he went straight round to his uncle's house and rescued his princess. Then he took the lamp from the sleeping Abanazar's hands and rubbed it. The Genie appeared again. WHOOSH!

48

"I am the Genie of the Lamp," she said. "What is your wish, oh master?"

"Please, Genie, can you take me and my princess home, and send that wicked Abanazar into outer space?"

"With pleasure," said the Genie, and with a puff of blue smoke she did just that.

From then on, Aladdin always kept the lamp with him, and he, his princess and his mum lived happily ever after. And whenever the night sky was clear they would look up at the stars and wonder what had happened to Uncle Abanazar.

"The End," Judy added.

"Well done, everyone!" said Max. "Bella?"

"What is your wish, oh master?" Bella asked him.

"Can I have my teapot back, please?"

THE END

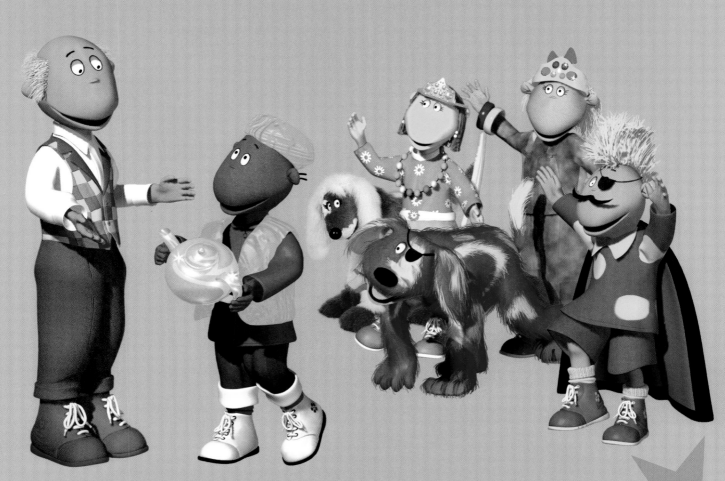

49

Who Shall We Be Today?

You will need round-ended scissors, safe glue
and a grown-up to help.
Milo and Fizz want to dress up as a clown and a fairy. Read the
words and look at the pictures to find out what they need. Cut them
out from the next page and glue them on Milo and Fizz.

Fizz the Fairy needs pink , a
sparkly , a pretty and a
for casting fairy spells.

Milo the Clown needs big ,
a flowery , a spotty ,
baggy and three to
juggle in the air.

50

51

Colour by Numbers

The Tweenies love dressing up!
Colour in this picture of them, using the numbers and
the colour chart to help you.

53

Be a Genie

Follow these instructions to make a genie's turban, then add bangles, sandals and baggy trousers gathered in at the ankles with sticky tape, and presto! You're a genie.

Ask a grown-up to help.

You will need:
String
Red card
Round-ended scissors
Sticky tape
Pencil
Rubber
Black pen
2 sheets of A4 white paper
Safe glue
Green card
Glitter
Ruler

1 Measure your head with a piece of string. Then cut out a piece of red card 4cm wide and slightly longer than your head measurement. Bend the card into a crown and tape the ends together.

2 To draw a turban, measure the width of your face with the string. Now draw three circles close together on the red card to make a triangular shape. Each circle should be half the width of your face.

3 Draw on some fabric folds with the black pen. Cut out the turban and tape it to the inside of the front of the crown. Rub out any pencil lines.

4 Draw and cut out two feather shapes from the red card. Draw a black line down the middle of each one. Snip the edges of the feathers with the scissors. Tape the ends of the feathers to the front of the turban.

5 Make a big green jewel by drawing a six-sided shape on the green card. Cut it out. Draw and cut out a smaller six-sided shape and glue it in the middle of the first. Draw lines with the black pen around the edges of the two shapes, then draw lines between the points of the larger shape and the points of the smaller shape, so it looks like a jewel. Add some glitter. Glue the jewel over the ends of the feathers.

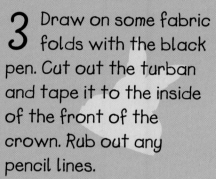

6 To make the beads, cut the A4 paper into narrow strips. Roll each strip around the pencil. Remove the rolled strips and glue them. Thread the beads onto string. Tape the string of beads across the turban and tape the ends to the back.

Jake's Fun Page
Hi! I'm Jake.

Join the dots to write my name.

Shiver my timbers! I'm pretending to be Jake the Pirate. Do you like my pirate ship? Can you see Milo the Pirate hiding on board? Colour the sails black.

The other Tweenies and I want to dress up as a knight, a chef, a builder and a wizard. Which four hats should we choose?

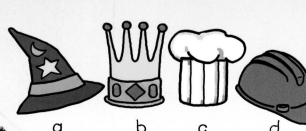

a   b   c   d   e   f

56

Answers: knight = e, chef = c, builder = d and wizard = a.

The Dressing-up Game

You will need a die and four pieces of costume for each player.

This is one of the Tweenies' favourite dressing-up games, and is perfect for two or more players.

Each player decides who they want to be, and chooses four things to wear as a costume. Then, each player chooses a number from one to six, for example, three. If they roll the die and get a three, they can put on a piece of their costume.

If they get any other number, they have to wait for their next turn to roll the die again. Players take it in turns to throw the die. The winner is the person who dresses up first.

surprise time

Woof woof!
I'm Doodles.
And
I'm Izzles.

Join the dots to write our names.

We love going to the park with the Tweenies.
Colour in this picture of us.

58

If you owned a puppy like me, what would you call it?

....

Write the name here.

It's Almost Time to Say Goodbye

It's almost time to say goodbye.
We hope you've enjoyed this Tweenies annual.
Here's a memory game to play.
See how well you do.

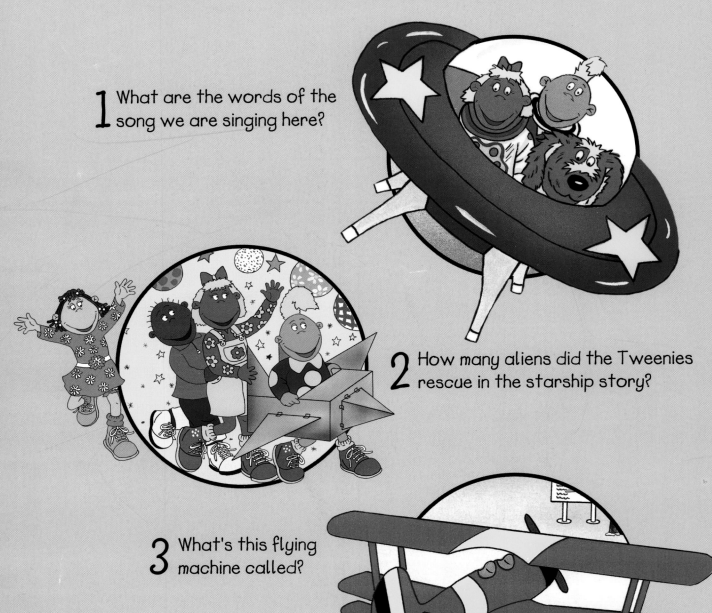

1 What are the words of the song we are singing here?

2 How many aliens did the Tweenies rescue in the starship story?

3 What's this flying machine called?

60

4 What's the name of this funny animal?

5 Which superhero rescued these flyers?

6 How did Doodles get up this tree? How did he get down?

7 Who is Jake pretending to be in this picture?

Here are the answers. How well did you do?

Space Race Board Game

This game is for two to four players.
You will need a counter for each player and a die.

It's going-home time! The Tweenies have been playing astronauts in space, but now they are racing back to planet Earth, where Max, Judy, Doodles and Izzles are waiting for them. Who will get home first?

Place your counters on the Start circles. Then take turns to throw the die and move your counters along the space tracks to Planet Earth – according to the number thrown. The player who reaches Earth first, with the right throw of the die, is the winner.

Start

Start

Plar